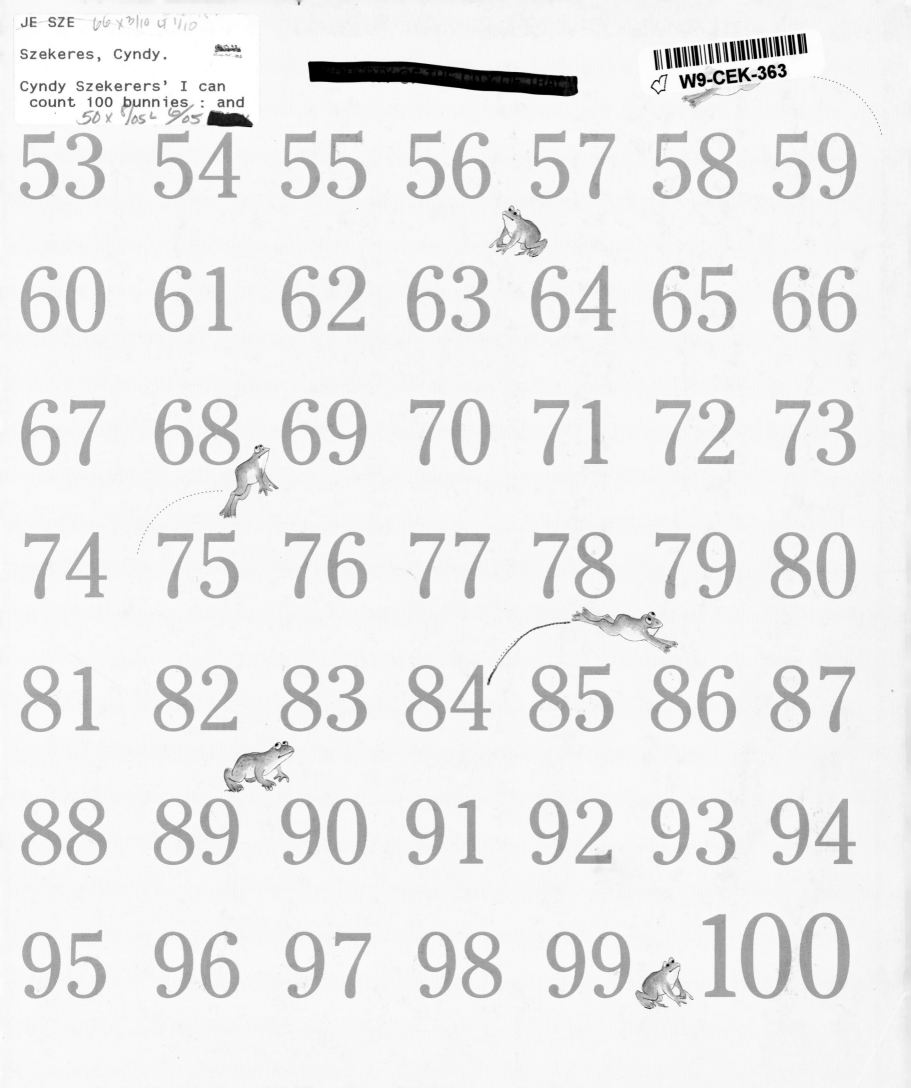

I Can Count
100 BUNNIES

And So Can You!

CYNDY SZEKERES'
I Can Count
100 BUNNIES

And So Can You!

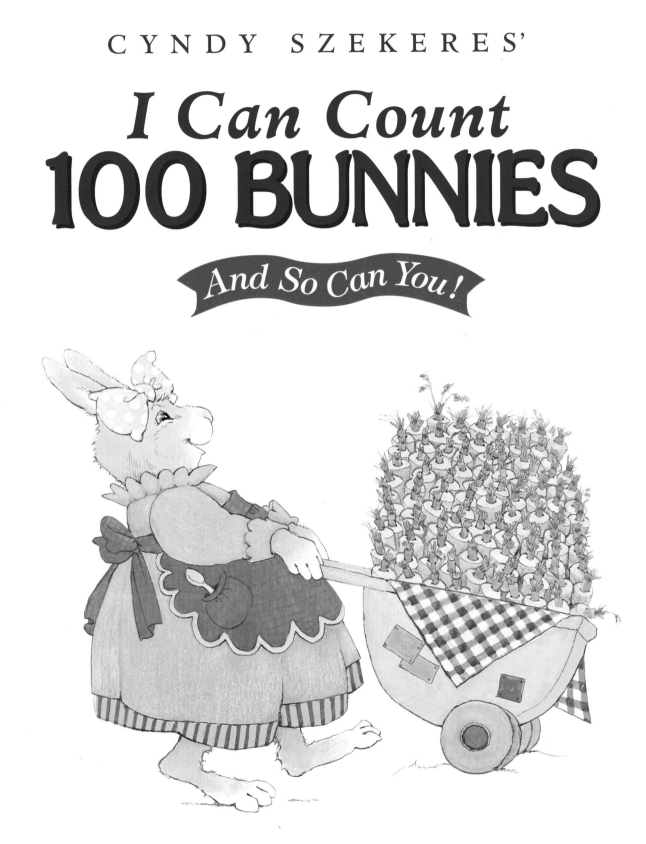

Cartwheel
B·O·O·K·S®

SCHOLASTIC INC.
New York   Toronto   London   Auckland   Sydney

Library of Congress Cataloging-in-Publication Data
Szekeres, Cyndy.
     I can count 100 bunnies — and so can you!/ Cyndy Szekeres.
        p.   cm.
     Summary: The reader is asked to count as more and more of Wilbur Bunny's
sisters and brothers, uncles, aunts, and cousins arrive to welcome the newest baby
bunny into the family.
     ISBN 0-590-38361-2
     [1. Rabbits — Fiction. 2. Counting.]   I. Title.
PZ7.S986Iae   1999
[E] — dc21   97-48904
                                                                                  CIP
                                                                                  AC

10   9   8   7   6   5   4   3   2   1   9/9   0/0   01   02   03

Printed in Singapore   46
First printing, February 1999

For
Nina
and
Emmett

❧

Gramma
loves
you both!

Wilbur is wearing his best pants and a new jacket.
Why is he so dressed up?
The 99 bunnies in his family will be gathering for a
special occasion. Wilbur wants to count them as they
arrive — and so can you! He counts himself first.
That's 1 bunny.

Wow! Look at this!
Here comes Mama with her special carrot cupcakes!
Papa is bringing out the party tables. The twins,
Pokey Nose and Nosey Blows, are helping.
They must be getting ready for something pretty
important!

Now we have 2, 3, 4, and 5 bunnies.

Wilbur's sisters help put out the folding chairs—
lots of them!
Here's Polly and Esther, Tosca and Nina, Patty and Cake.

That will be 6, 7, 8, 9, 10, 11 bunnies.

Oh, dear me!
Wilbur's big brothers are carrying too many cups
of juice!
There's Obediah, Jeremiah...

Joshua and Jack. Oops!
They make 12, 13, 14, and 15 bunnies.

More brothers have to bring more paper cups and juice. Here come Ben, Bobby, Bartholomew, Marco, and Zac. Now it's cleanup time—and the party hasn't even begun!

We now have 16, 17, 18, 19, 20 bunnies.

The aunties arrive in their party clothes! Don't they look pretty?
Auntie Peggy, Auntie Polly, Auntie Pasto, Auntie Lou, and Auntie Prunella!

21 22 23 24

25

Count 21, 22, 23, 24, 25 bunnies.

Also, Great-aunt Josie, Great-aunt Rosie, Great-aunt
Posie, Great-aunt Pew, and Great-aunt Louella.
Don't stop counting!

Wow—26, 27, 28, 29, 30 bunnies!
Wilbur has a very big family.

This is going to be a big party!
Grandma and Grandpa arrive with some grandbunnies—
Willy and Nilly, Freddy and Betty, Bumpy and Bea.

Count 31, 32, 33, 34, 35, 36, 37, 38 bunnies!

Cousins Merty, Gerty, Dotty, and Dee bring lots of colorful balloons!

That makes **39, 40, 41, 42** bunnies.

Grandpa made whistles for all the little bunnies.
More noisy cousins arrive, hooting and tooting.
Tweet, twonk, twank...toowoo!

They toot their thanks to Grandpa. There's Randy Radish, Hopping John, Barbara Bushytail, Dancing Don, Peter Pussytoes, and Bump-a-long Billie.

Count 43, 44, 45, 46, 47, 48 bunnies.

Nelly Smelly Rose, Tommy and Tilly, Wendy Wide-Awake, Pasta and Fazoo, Jimmie Jiggletoes, and Sulky Sue all have whistles, too!

They make 53 54 55 56

They make 49, 50, 51, 52, 53, 54, 55, 56 bunnies...
and more are still coming!

Yum! Something smells good. The uncles are here carrying casseroles.
There's Uncle Howard, Uncle Lester, Uncle Dave and Uncle Chester,

57 58 59 60

Uncle Buster, Uncle Caesar, and Uncles Ralph and Ebeneezer.

Now there are 57, 58, 59, 60, 61, 62, 63, 64 bunnies!

Uncle Charlie, Uncle Chubby,
Uncle Chuck and Uncle Blubby,
Uncle Randall, Uncle Rick,
Uncle Don and Uncle Dick…
and let's not forget Great-uncle Hercules!
What's the big occasion?

Count 65, 66, 67, 68, 69, 70, 71, 72, 73 bunnies.
Oh my!

The teenage cousins arrive—one for every letter of the alphabet!
There's **A**ndrea, **B**everly, **C**hristopher, and **D**olly,
Emmett, **F**rancis, **G**racie, and **H**olly…

Now 74, 75, 76, 77, 78, 79, 80, 81 bunnies are ready to party!

Some Alphabet bunnies like sports.
There's **Ida**, **Jessie**, **Kevin**, and **Larry**,
Melanie, **Nancy**, **Otis**, and **Perry**.

82

83

84

85

That's 82, 83, 84, 85, 86, 87, 88, 89 bunnies.

Quincy and **R**asputin, **S**am and **T**om Tootin,
Ursula, **V**ictor, **W**anda, **X**erxes and **Y**olanda…
and **Z**enobia!

Count 90, 91, 92, 93, 94, 95, 96, 97, 98, 99 bunnies!
They've all arrived! Or have they?

Can you count all 99 bunnies?

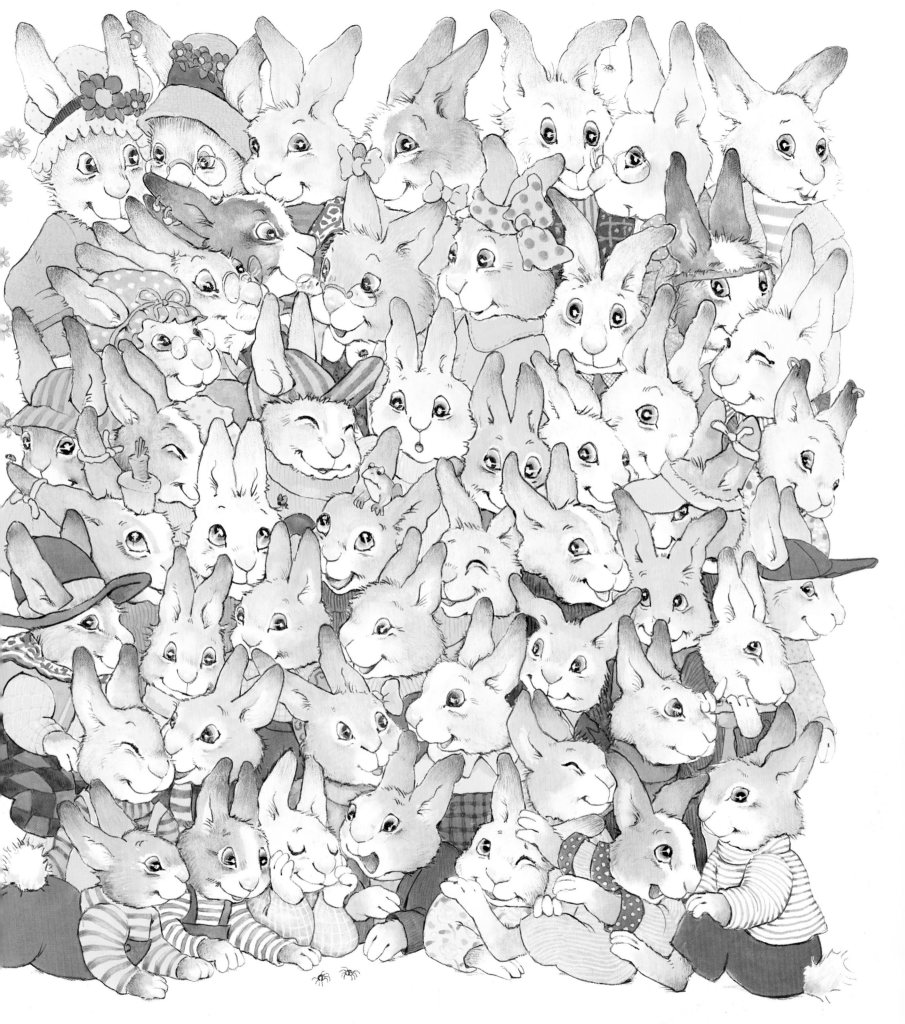

What do you think they've gathered here to celebrate?

It's the arrival of Wilbur's new baby
sister — Sweet Petunia.
Now Wilbur can count to 100 —
and so can you!
Hip, hip, hooray!
It's time for the party!

100